The Legend of Leelanau

By Kathy-jo Wargin
Illustrated by Gijsbert van Frankenhuyzen

Sleeping Bear Press

This book was so fun to do and as usual I could not have done it without my models. Sally Charness posed as the young Indian maiden, Leelinau. Her every movement was elegant and each expression magical. She brought an innocence and enchantment to the character. Five year-old Annie Boylan Fanta was the body double for the fairies. With her gymnastic skills and pixie-like body, she was a natural for all the flying, floating, and twirling she had to perform. I can honestly say that no one but little Annie could have brought such animation to the fairies. Finally, many thanks to Jane and Geoffrey Gamble, who lifted, tossed, and twirled Annie into every possible fairy position imaginable. You are all great neighbors. Thank you.

—*Gijsbert*

I would like to thank all those who helped during the course of researching the different versions of this tale, in particular Tom and Kathy Baker of Calumet, Michigan, Historian Wil Shapton, John Boatman, American Indian Studies at the University of Wisconsin-Milwaukee, and the many others who provided their own versions of this Leelinau tale. I would also like to thank Carol and Jim Kelly, for their unwavering belief, my husband Ed, for contributing his talent and insight, and my son Jake, for always listening to my stories, and sharing his youthful point of view with me. And last but not least, my dog Salmon, who keeps my feet warm whenever I work at my desk.

This book is dedicated to us all—
may we recognize and treasure the child that lives in each of us.

—*Kathy-jo*

Text copyright © 2003 Kathy-jo Wargin
Illustration copyright © 2003 Gijsbert van Frankenhuyzen

Sleeping Bear Press
310 North Main Street
Chelsea, MI 48118
www.sleepingbearpress.com

Sleeping Bear Press is an imprint of The Gale Group, Inc., a division of Thomson Learning, Inc.

Printed and bound in Canada.

10 9 8 7 6 5 4 3 2 1

Library of Congress Cataloging-in-Publication Data on file.
ISBN: 1-58536-150-X

About The Legend of Leelanau

Henry Rowe Schoolcraft (1793 – 1864) was an explorer, Indian Agent, and Superintendent of Indian Affairs in Michigan from 1836 to 1841. During his time in the Great Lakes region, he collected legends, lore, and valuable information from the Native American cultures he lived with. In 1822 he married Jane Johnston, daughter of an Ojibwe woman named *Ozha-guscoday-way-quay* and an Irish Fur Trader named John Johnston. Jane Johnston and her Ojibwe family assisted Schoolcraft in the collection, interpretation, and transcription of his essays.

The Legend of Leelanau was originally transcribed by Schoolcraft as *Leelinau, or The Lost Daughter.* For me, researching this legend became an interesting study in migration and evolution of stories and ideas. Today, there are different versions of this tale, yet many still possess root characteristics of both versions Schoolcraft published in the 1800's. In the first of Schoolcraft's versions, the story begins in Kaug Wudjoo, now known as the Porcupine Mountains. In the other, Kaug Wudjoo was changed to Naigow Wudjoo, or the Grand Sable Dunes.

In his transcription of the tale, the young girl was given the birth name of Neenizu, or "my dear life" but was called Leelinau. It is interesting to me that Schoolcraft possibly adored the idea of this delightful child Leelinau so much that he used her name when naming Leelanau County, which many refer to as the Land of Delight. Other versions of this tale have become known as the Legend of Little Girl's Point.

Human nature makes it rare for the same story to be told in identical fashion repeatedly. I encourage you to discover the many versions of this wonderful tale and others. Compare them, retell them, get to know them. Ask elders about their childhood stories and become familiar with them, before they are lost forever. Here is my version of Leelinau, may her spirit guide you to the land of delight and the innocence of childhood.

— *Kathy-jo Wargin*

Long ago in a land of great lakes, there lived
a maiden named Leelinau. She lived where hills
of sand drifted between water and sky, not far
from a dark and mysterious forest.

This forest was tangled with trees
and vines, and it smelled rich like the
earth. Leelinau's grandparents, and
their grandparents before them, always
knew of this place as the Spirit Wood.

Although it was beautiful, most people
were afraid to enter the Spirit Wood because
of the Pukwudjininees who lived there.

The Pukwudjininees were tiny fairies
of the forest, and known to play friendly
but mischievous tricks on people.

These fairies were rarely seen by others because they could vanish behind trees whenever they wanted to. Still, everyone knew they were real because the sound of their laughter would float through the air like bells being tossed in the wind. And then always, as fast as it came, it would be gone.

During the day the fairies snatched whitefish from drying racks and stole berries from woven baskets. They took feathers from the headbands of sleeping men, and hid canoe paddles high up in the trees.

At night, when the village was asleep, they skipped through the Spirit Wood and went to the great lake. Here, as the moon cast silver-shine upon the shore, the fairies rode upon the backs of bears and danced merrily upon the sand. When they were satisfied with their fun, they crept back into the Spirit Wood to sleep in the antlers of resting deer.

Most people were afraid of the Pukwudjininees and the Spirit Wood, but not Leelinau. She loved the Spirit Wood more than anything else and was drawn to its most hidden places, always searching for the longest paths to follow.

While in the Spirit Wood,
Leelinau climbed the tallest
trees and hung from their
branches, bending them
downwards as she jumped
to the forest floor. She
used fallen trees for secret
bridges, stepping carefully
along the way.

Leelinau gave her animal friends
necklaces made from colorful seeds,
and played hide and seek with the red
fox. She made braids with forest grasses,
weaving them round to make sturdy
nests for mother birds. Sometimes she
would make herself a soft bed out of
leaves and ferns, and lay down to rest.

One day, when Leelinau
returned home from the
Spirit Wood, her mother and
father said "Leelinau, you
must not go into the Spirit
Wood. The Pukwudjininees
live there, and they are full
of mischief. They will be
sure to cast a spell and
carry you away for good!"

Leelinau did not look
at her mother and father,
she did not like what they
were saying.

When Leelinau woke the next day, she tried not to think about the Spirit Wood. She was forbidden to go there, yet she could not resist the longing that seemed to pull her there. Leelinau walked quietly to the edge of the forest. Before she knew it, she was running as fast as she could. It did not take long to forget about her parents and their warning.

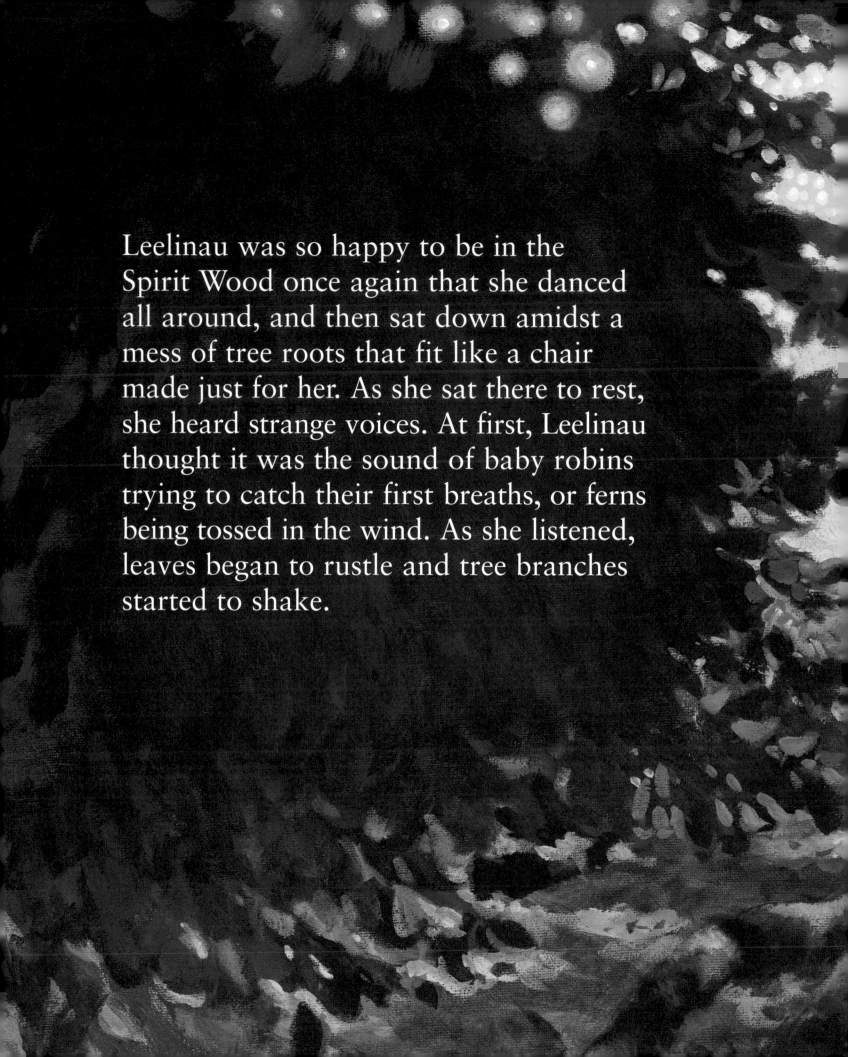

Leelinau was so happy to be in the Spirit Wood once again that she danced all around, and then sat down amidst a mess of tree roots that fit like a chair made just for her. As she sat there to rest, she heard strange voices. At first, Leelinau thought it was the sound of baby robins trying to catch their first breaths, or ferns being tossed in the wind. As she listened, leaves began to rustle and tree branches started to shake.

One by one, Pukwudjininees were coming from everywhere in the forest! They came from beneath roots of trees, they came from inside flowers, they came from tiny forest paths and climbed out of robin's nests, saying,

"We dance upon the forest paths
we sing beneath the trees,
our sweet and gentle laughter floats
like bells upon the breeze.

Why don't you stay a little while
before it's much too late?
Today you are a tender child
and time will never wait."

Leelinau joined hands with the fairy people and romped through the forest all day. They fed raspberries to black bears, and played games with a jumping mouse. They were having such a wonderful time that Leelinau almost forgot to go home.

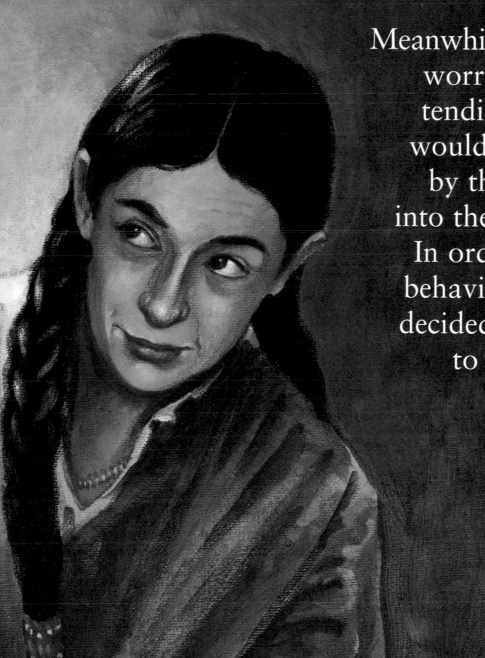

When Leelinau returned, her parents said, "Leelinau, you disobeyed us. We forbid you to go into the Spirit Wood and yet you returned there. Why is this so? Why must you disobey us? There are Pukwudjininees in the Spirit Wood, and they will cast a spell on you! Leelinau, you must not return there ever again."

Meanwhile, Leelinau's parents worried that she was not tending to her work, and would be enchanted away by the fairies if she went into the Spirit Wood again. In order to keep her from behaving so foolishly, they decided it was time for her to marry a young man from the village.

Leelinau did not want to be married, she did not want to grow up so soon. When her parents told her she would be happy with her new husband, she did not believe them. Leelinau smiled softly, but the smile was only pretend.

On her wedding day, the women of the village prepared Leelinau for the ceremony. Her dress was white with tender pink beads, and she wore a crown of twigs and flowers in her hair.

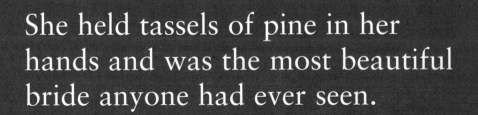

She held tassels of pine in her hands and was the most beautiful bride anyone had ever seen.

Moments before the wedding, Leelinau
went to her father and pleaded, "Oh dear
father, before I am married, may I walk
through the Spirit Wood one last time?"
Leelinau's father did not think this was
a good idea, but Leelinau drew her chin
downward and looked sweet, and he
could not resist his lovely daughter.

When no one was looking, Leelinau vanished into the Spirit Wood. As she skipped along, her heart felt lighter. When she reached the center of the forest, the Pukwudjininees were there, and they said,

"Come dance upon the forest paths
come sing among the trees,
come let your gentle laughter float
like bells upon the breeze.

Please say that you will stay with us
before it's much too late
to live forever as a child
while life beyond must wait."

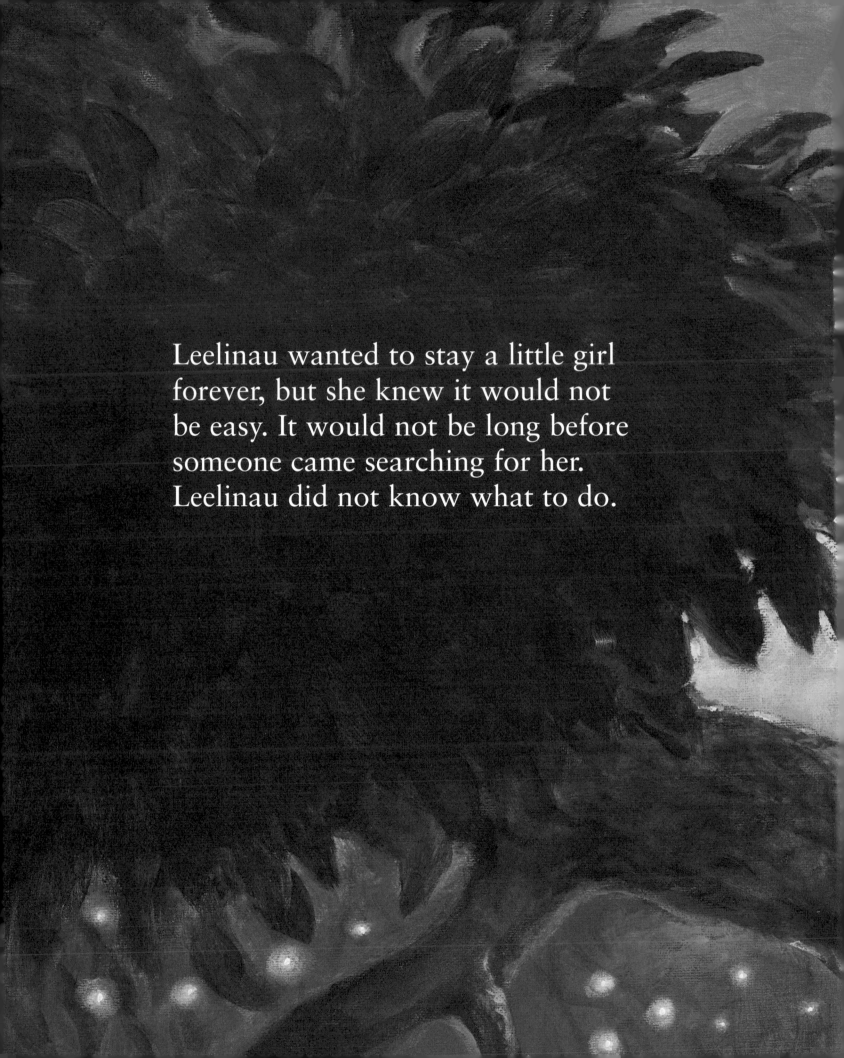

Leelinau wanted to stay a little girl forever, but she knew it would not be easy. It would not be long before someone came searching for her. Leelinau did not know what to do.

Stephenson

Ingalls

Wallace

Menominee

B a y

ROCK I.

WASHINGTON
ISLAND

DOOR

Sturgeon
Bay

L A K E   M I C

A & W

Algoma

sco Jc.

UNEE

JUN 2 6 2003

Kewaunee

Kathy-jo Wargin

Author Kathy-jo Wargin has earned national recognition as a children's author by bringing old tales to life. Her books include award-winning titles such as *The Legend of Sleeping Bear*, *The Legend of Mackinac Island*, *The Legend of the Loon*, *The Legend of the Lady's Slipper*, *The Michigan Counting Book*, *L is for Lincoln: An Illinois Alphabet*, *The Michigan Reader for Boys and Girls*, and many others.

Kathy-jo and husband, photographer Ed Wargin, live in Petoskey, Michigan with their son Jake and family dog Salmon. Ms. Wargin is a frequent guest speaker at many reading conferences throughout the country and conducts writing workshops and group presentations for adults and children.

Gijsbert van Frankenhuyzen

Gijsbert was born in the Netherlands. Always drawing as a young boy, his father encouraged Gijsbert to make art his career. After high school, he attended and graduated from the Royal Academy of Arts in Arnhem. He immigrated to America in 1976 and worked as Art Director for the *Michigan Natural Resources Magazine* for 17 years. Gijsbert now paints full time and loves the freedom of painting whatever he wants.

The Legend of Leelanau is his twelfth children's book with Sleeping Bear Press. His other titles include *The Legend of Sleeping Bear, Adopted by an Owl*, and most recently *Jam & Jelly by Holly & Nellie*.

Gijsbert and his family live in Bath, Michigan, where they share their 40-acre farm with sheep, horses, dogs, cats, turkeys, rabbits, chickens, and pigeons. They also provide a temporary home for many orphaned and injured wildlife. The farm, the land, and the animals make great subjects for him to paint.

I dance upon the forest paths,
I sing beneath the trees,
I let my gentle laughter float
like bells upon the breeze.

So hold this secret in your heart
before it's much too late,
children are the truest joy
and time will never wait.

For childhood passes much too fast,
it never lingers on,
just like the sound of lovely bells,
it comes — and then it's gone.

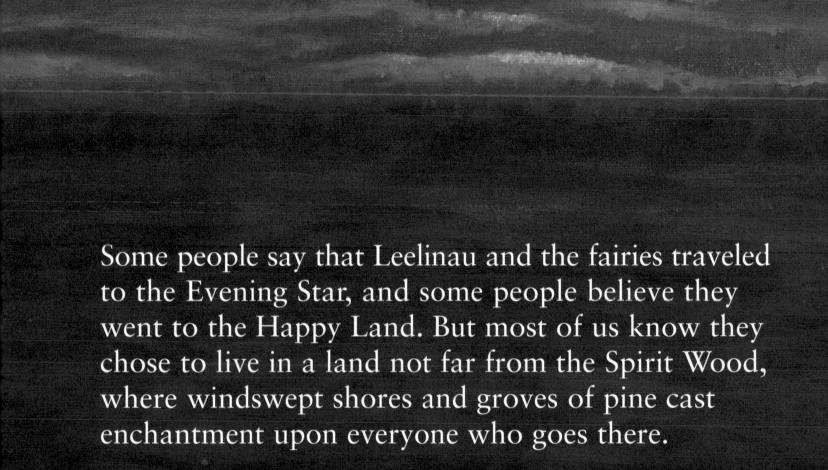

Some people say that Leelinau and the fairies traveled to the Evening Star, and some people believe they went to the Happy Land. But most of us know they chose to live in a land not far from the Spirit Wood, where windswept shores and groves of pine cast enchantment upon everyone who goes there.

Many years ago, when explorer Henry Rowe Schoolcraft set out to name this place, he called it Leelanau, perhaps naming it for the lovely girl that had enchanted him in a story long before. Today, this magical place is known as Leelanau, the land of delight, where all who believe in the maiden Leelinau will feel her words and laughter forever.

Right then, everyone
knew Leelinau chose to run
away with the Pukwudjininees
and remain a little girl forever.
They understood that childhood
was like the laughter of fairies,
filling your heart with the
sound of a million bells, and that
as fast as it comes, it's gone.

And there, as the fisherman was
speaking, the sound of silver bells
filled the air, surrounding everyone
with music and a young girl's voice,

"I want to dance on forest paths
and sing among the trees,
I want to hear my laughter float
like bells upon the breeze.

So I must go away from here,
there is no time to wait,
to live where I'll remain a child
before it's much too late.

For childhood passes much too fast,
it never lingers on,
just like the sound of lovely bells,
it comes and then it's gone."

Just then, a lone fisherman walked into the village. He said that late the night before, he saw a beautiful princess dancing along the shore with fairies at her side, and it was the happiest sight he had ever seen.

Back at the village, the wedding ceremony was ready to begin, but Leelinau was nowhere to be found. Leelinau's family and the rest of the village waited quietly. They waited so long the hot flames of the wedding fire turned to cool white ashes.

Leelinau's parents lowered their heads with sadness. They were sorry they wished for their daughter to grow up so soon. Now, their only wish was to have her back for one more day.